Huda Alkhamis

CLOCK BEATS

AUSTIN MACAULEY PUBLISHERS™
LONDON • CAMBRIDGE • NEW YORK • SHARJAH

ISBN – 9789948796787 – (Paperback)
ISBN – 9789948796794 – (E-Book)

Application Number: MC-10-01-2387696
Age Classification: 13+

Printer Name: iPrint Global Ltd
Printer Address: Witchford, England

First Published 2023
AUSTIN MACAULEY PUBLISHERS FZE
Sharjah Publishing City
P.O Box [519201]
Sharjah, UAE
www.austinmacauley.ae
+971 655 95 202

Season One

Introduction

How can I change the stress and the sadness I face in life into a great event? How can I allow myself to accept the absence of my loved one? How can I accept the fact that my loved one passed away? How can I honor my loved ones with my accomplishments and my successes? How can I live my life without the negative impact of losing my loved one? I cannot tolerate it. No more. No more.

What is life? What is pain? How are the feelings of losing someone? How are the feelings of being the cause of someone's death? How can a human tolerate this type of pain, losing someone? How can a human tolerate this type of pain, missing someone? How can a human tolerate this type of pain, wishing to hug their loved one for the last time, one more hug, just one more time?

Life is like a plane. You fly this plane wherever you want to. This plane works upon your orders. This plane works upon your desire. This plane works upon your permission. But what makes this plane fall? As you know, each plane happens to have unexpected mechanical problems. For this time, the plane which acts as our life has a certain mechanical problem which is our destiny. From birth, each human has a written destiny. This destiny is written by God. We as human beings cannot do anything about it. Perhaps, we can work hard to be rich. Perhaps, we can study to assist each other in life matters. Perhaps, we can feed hungry people by providing them some food. Perhaps, we can provide thirsty people with some water. But destiny, we cannot change it.

Destiny of the other world or what we call death is a certain fact that has to happen at a particular time during our life's journey. I am one of those people who lost their loved ones. I am one of those people who cry on a dead body. I am one of those people who tried in vain to wake up a dead body. I am missing the love of my life. I feel lonely. All I am waiting for is a call from heaven for my spirit to gather with my loved one's spirit.

Eighteen complete chapters will discuss my story of losing my loved one. Those chapters are full of pain and regret. Those chapters might touch something in your soul. But that is okay because we are human beings. We laugh, we cry, and we have to accept the past as an event that happened. We have to accept the past and live with it. We have to promise ourselves that we are able to accept the pain and honor our loved ones with whatever success we create. I am sure we all can do that.

Chapter One

Two friends fell in love with each other. Rich abandoned the love of his life, Mond, without any reason. Mond got shocked by her lover's abandonment. She got sad and she had terrible thoughts that he left her because he was in a relationship with her best friend, Zola. Mond blamed her friend that she caused that abandonment.

Although Mond had to struggle for a period of time, she got strong, and she decided to pursue her degree. Mond chose to enroll in medical school. She was successfully accepted in a medical school. She got employed in a hospital. It was not easy for the doctor to forget the pain of the abandonment caused by her boyfriend. Doctor Mond truly believed in her potential that she could go on in her life. The doctor truly believed in her strengths that she could create her success and let it last forever. The doctor truly believed in her goals and knew how to bring them into reality. She truly believed in herself.

Knowing all those factors, she successfully joined a hospital with a great medical team. The doctor was specialized in medication. She was well known in that hospital. Patients came from all across the country to be diagnosed under this doctor's supervision. The days passed and she became famous for her profession. The management of the hospital trusted her to manage the department. The management of the hospital trusted her to hold two hours clinic on daily basis.

In this clinic, Doctor Mond managed to meet patients with different backgrounds to provide them with proper treatment. Now that she managed to show her potential of applying the skills she learned in medical school, she was able to cure her soul of losing and missing the love of her life. She still broke down a bit when she saw her pictures with him. She still remembered that they both made the promise to go to medical school. She still remembered that they both had shared goals. She believed she must be successful in whatever profession she held. She realized the importance of success for a human being. She realized the impact on her soul of this abandonment.

It was clear for her that the hospital's life brought joy and peace for her broken soul. It was clear for her that helping patients bring goodness and blessings. It was clear for her that supporting sick people was great work and a rewarding one. The daily working routine was a wonderful experience for her. She did great work to manage her time and getting to the hospital in the early morning and in every day.

Clearly, the doctor's potential was a mirror for her long-lasting honest feelings toward supporting patients of different diseases. The more the doctor met the patient in her clinic, the more calm and peaceful feelings hit her friendly soul. That soul was the exact soul of the same person who was injured deeply when the love of her life decided to abandon her.

Would it be possible for the doctor to remove the hurting chapter from her life? That chapter of her falling in love with her boyfriend. The chapter of her losing the love of her life. The chapter of her wishing just wishing to know the unknown to really decide what to do, when to do it, and how to do it.

What made Doctor Mond able to tolerate all this pain is that she had strong faith that God had planned everything in our lives and we as human beings should accept that as destiny. The doctor believed that accepting the pain was an essential part of the success cycle. Doctor Mond understood that any person who sought and strived for success would surely face some type of pain and challenge.

Those challenges can either quit someone's life or allow that person to really dive deep into those challenges and build success. Doctor Mond did not share her pain of losing the love of her life to her colleagues at work. The doctor knew that some people do not sympathize with a person who got problems in their life. People might throw jokes and hurt the person who speaks up his thoughts. Doctor Mond decided to leave her sad story behind her and only focus and enjoy supporting patients at the hospital.

Chapter Two

One day, Doctor Mond finished her duty at the hospital. The clock rang to announce the time as 11:00 p.m. She was about to checkout and leave the hospital. She heard the call for patient resistance or what was called 'Code Blue.' One nurse was running to the nursing station asking for assistance. The nurse mentioned a patient's name that is familiar to Doctor Mond. After hearing the patient's name, Doctor Mond decided to wait until all the doctors install the machines, in that patient's body, to wake him up. The patient was unconscious. The attendant doctor recorded in the patient's file that this patient arrived at the hospital at 11:00 p.m. and was in a coma.

With a quick movement in providing the necessary needs for the patient, the doctors successfully installed wires and oxygen for this patient. The doctors left the room heading to the nursing station. The attendant doctor advised the nurses to make sure that this patient must be under oxygen until the next morning. The nurses file the doctor's notes and the attendant doctor checked out.

Doctor Mond looked behind her and she made sure the corridor is safe to pass. With slow steps, Doctor Mond started to read the room number. Doctor Mond felt intense worry for whom she would see when she would open the door. Doctor Mond accessed the room. The room was dark enough that the doctor almost saw nothing. Doctor Mond started to inhale and exhale deeply. Doctor Mond reached the patient room. The doctor did not hear anything but the breaths of the patient sceeth, sceeth, sceeth (breath sound). The patient's lungs were deeply damaged.

Doctor Mond looked at the white bedsheets over the bed. She was standing close to the patient's legs side. She placed her hand lightly on the bedsheet sensing the patient's legs and moved along to the patient's head. She recognized the one who was laying down on the bed. He was the love of her life. The one who abandoned her years ago.

Doctor Mond started to shed some tears and said, "Oh no, God no. This is impossible. It is him! It is him! It is him!"

Doctor Mond got close to the patient and tried to wake him up. She started to tilt his head. With closed dizzy eyes, the patient was speechless. Doctor Mond felt weak, and she did not know what to do. Doctor Mond was about to lose her mind. She was crying deeply.

She opened her gown preparing to take it off. She opened her hair trying to let it loose and settle over her shoulders. She removed her stethoscope and put it over the patient's table. Doctor Mond laid down her body (her chest) on the patient's chest (her lover). After that, she started crying.

Although the patient was in a coma and because of her severity of crying, he started to wake up and sensed her presence. The patient tried to say something. He finally said, "Who is this? I think I know this body." The patient tried to raise his arm. He raised his arm and placed it over Doctor's

Mond head. The patient sensed her hair. The patient took a deep breath. The patient kept touching her hair.

Doctor Mond started crying and crying and crying. The doctor said nothing but kept crying. She tried to lift her body from the lover's body, the patient. Again, he hardly lifted his hand, and he lightly touched her hair with his weak fingers. He asked the doctor, "Who are you? I think I know this body. Who are you? I think I've touched this hair before. Who are you? Who are you? Please tell me who are you?"

Doctor Mond kept crying and crying. She said, "I cannot tell you who I am. Please let me go. Please let me go. Please let me go."

She noticed that dawn time was about to approach, and the next shift of the medical team was about to start. The doctor realized that she needed to leave as soon as she could. She did not want the other doctors and the nurses to see her in the patient's room. Doctor Mond did not want them to question her. She did not want anyone to discover the relationship between her and the patient.

She did not want the whole hospital to know that the patient who was in a coma was the love of her life. She decided to leave the room. With trembling hands, she tied her hair. She wore her gown, and she left the room. She sadly forgot her stethoscope.

It was not planned for the doctor to meet up with the love of her life. It was not planned for the doctor to cross the lines and access the patient's room when her duty is finished. It was not planned for the doctor to unplug wires and machines from the patient's body.

Would it be the final season for the two couples to say goodbye to each other? Would it be the final kiss for the two couples to officially lose each other? Now that the patient had no strengths. Now that the patient had no clue who was the person who came to his room. Now that the patient had no clue who unplugged the wires and the machines from his body. Who is a mistake is this?

Will the patient sustain until the next shift of nurses and doctors check-in and install the wires on his body to help him stay alive? The doctor left the room. The machines were beeping. The patient started to develop harsh pain in his chest that he could not breathe normally. The patient needed to be oxygenated.

The patient's heart was slowing down bit by bit. The patient started to struggle, and he could not breathe. After all the efforts for the doctors the night before to wake the patient's heart, Doctor Mond, the love of his life, unplugged the machines from his body.

The doctor was in shock seeing the love of her life in front of her in a critical situation. The doctor was in shock hearing the name of the love of her life along with the code blue. The doctor could not sustain not to go, and check if he the love of her life that was coded. The doctor could not sustain seeing the love of her life in front of her without hugging him tightly.

She left the patient's room without realizing that she did not plug the wires and machines. She left the patient's room without realizing that she forgot to take her stethoscope. It was not a planned meeting between the two couples. What a sad ending between the doctor and the love of her life.

She was approaching to leave the room. She was opening the door and going out of the room. The door was shut quite hard. The patient had no strength to call the nursing station. He had no strength to lift his body. He had no strength to press the bell to notify the nurses in the nursing station that he needed assistance. The patient was barely breathing. The patient could not survive for the night that he realized that he was trying in vain. No one was around the patient to support his critical health situation.

Chapter Three

The female doctor went home. She tried to sleep but she could not. The sun was shining. The birds were singing. The morning was approaching, Doctor Mond's phone was ringing. It was the hospital. Doctor Mond had an emergency call from the manager of the hospital. The hospital is calling her for an immediate meeting.

Doctor Mond went to the hospital. She met with the manager of the hospital. The manager of the hospital asked her where she was last night. The doctor answered that she finished her shift and she left home. The manager of the hospital looked her in the eyes, and he said, "Why do you lie? If you did not stay at the hospital last night, then may I see your stethoscope?"

Doctor Mond panicked, and she looked at her gown. She did not find the stethoscope. She said, "Perhaps I forgot it in my car or left it at home."

The manager of the hospital repeated, "Why do you lie? What you did last night was unethical. What you did last night was not expected from you. You shocked me. The nursing and doctors in the morning shift found your stethoscope in room number A420. Not only that, the nurse and the doctor reported to me this early morning that they found the patient in his room dead. Do you know why this happened to this patient? Wires and machines were not plugged into his body. The patient was struggling for long hours. The patient was looking for a way to breathe in vain." The manager of the hospital blamed the doctor for why she left her stethoscope in the patient's room. The manager of the hospital blamed the doctor for why she tried to kill this patient. The patient that was in a coma?

Of course, the manager of the hospital did not know the relation between that couple. The manager of the hospital did not wait for her response. He directly submitted a request for the billing department to finish up any finances for Doctor Mond. The manager of the hospital fired Doctor Mond accusing her that he thought she purposely tried to kill the patient. Which is unethical for her to be a doctor doing this.

Doctor Mond went silent for a minute. She felt breathless. The doctor felt dizzy and fatigue. The doctor now was hopeless. The doctor now was broken into pieces. The doctor stood and asked the manager of the hospital to excuse her. Doctor Mond left the manager's office. The doctor headed to her office to collect her certificates preparing to leave the place of her rewarding work, the hospital.

Doctor Mond went home. She stayed silent for days. The doctor felt guilty for killing the love of her life.

After harsh days and sleepless nights, Doctor Mond decided to apply for work in another hospital. Because the doctor was a hard working person, she had the chance to join a new medical team in another hospital. Doctor Mond was happy that she would be able to support the patients in the hospital. The doctor prepared herself for the new challenge.

The doctor learned that it was alright to feel guilty and accept the pain of it. The doctor learned that things happen, and she is a human of hopes and goals that she should go on in her life. The doctor was full of self-motivation that she was able to accept the past and proceed with her new rewarding work.

All the medical teams in the new hospital engaged with the doctor's lifestyle. All the medical team in the new hospital liked the doctor's joyful character. Doctor Mond was able to blend in with the new environment.

In shinny day full of bright sunshine, the sky was blue. The birds were singing. Doctor Mond woke up and decided to go for a walk. The doctor headed to the kitchen. She refilled her bottle of water. She grabbed her bottle of water. Doctor Mond dressed up and went to the nearest garden.

Doctor Mond started to walk. Seeing the blue sky and hearing the birds' singing, Doctor Mond said, "What a wonderful morning. What a calm blue sky. What a great day. One full hour of joyful feeling is the result of this walking hour."

The doctor looked at the sky and raised her arms and screamed, "God, I miss him. God, I need him. God, please accept my apology and forgive me if I was the cause for the love of my life to pass away. God, help me to honor my rewarding work to the soul of the love of my life. I love him. I love him. I love him so much."

Chapter Four

The doctor was fired. She completed her life normally. She decided to work in another hospital, and she started, and it was a fresh start for her.

Doctor Mond was pleased to meet the new medical team. It was a chance for Doctor Mond to shape her experience and beat any challenges she ever faces.

One day, one patient knocked on Doctor Mond's clinic door. She said, "Welcome, come in." When the patient opened the door, Doctor Mond stood, and she was shocked. She said, "You!" Doctor Mond welcomed the patient to sit. The doctor had many thoughts about this patient.

Doctor Mond started to quickly brainstorm who that patient was. She started to quickly question herself in the middle of hundreds of thoughts. *Is he my aaa, uh, no, no he must be another person? I must be tired enough to have these thoughts.*

Doctor Mond was standing near her desk. She was speechless. She started to lose her focus.

The patient was standing near the door. The patient was reluctant to enter the clinic because of the doctor's facial expressions. Doctor Mond could not sustain to keep up her sights on the patient's face. The doctor started to move on her reports on top of her desk. She started to do random movements to really avoid her sights to drill into this patient's face.

Of course, the patient could not take a step further to take a seat. The patient felt worried from what he saw. Minutes are passing and hearts are beating. Both Doctor Mond and the patient started to hear the clock's sound due to this heavy silence. Doctor Mond started to sweat that she started to remember detailed moments between her and the love of her life.

The patient started to hear the doctor's breath huh huh (breathing sound). Breath in, breath out. Although the office door was opened, the patient raised his hand and slightly knocked on the door one more time. He did that because he wanted to clear the distracted mind of this doctor.

After the patient knocked on the door, the doctor felt calm and slowly raised her face and opened her eyes. The doctor took a deep breath and she repeated, "You are welcome, please come on in." The patient looked at the doctor's eyes. He tilted his head right. He tilted his head left.

He smiled and he said, "Happy to see you, doctor. It has been a long journey for both of us. It has been a long journey full of pains. It has been a long journey full of challenges. It has been years of abundance." The patient said, "I am sure it was not a good ten years for both of us. Here I am! A person with hope and goals. A person who puts a promise and never settles until building a great future. Here I am the same person. Here I am the same soul. Here I am the person who is proud to see his best friend pursuing her goals. Here you are a doctor. As if you meant to be a doctor. You promised to be a doctor and look at you now, now you are a doctor. I have a lot to say. But I feel thirsty. May I have a cup of water? We really have a lot to talk about."

Doctor Mond was listening to this patient. She was looking at him but not hearing him. She was looking at his lips. The lips that were meant to be for her only. The sound of his voice felt so calming to her.

Doctor Mond felt the pain of the abundance ends. The doctor started to breathe deeply. She deeply wanted to touch this patient to make sure he was alive. She wanted to make sure he did not die.

Chapter Five

The patient entered the doctor's clinic. He was surprised by the doctor's facial expression. He sat down and she sat down. She tried to hold herself. She took a deep breath. She looked at his file. She looked at his eyes. She went in silence. She went in silence. She went in silence.

She had tears from her eyes. She said, "Excuse me, I need to bring something to the clinic." She went to the office's files. She gave the patient her back. She opened one file. That file was of his pictures. She tried to see if the patient looked similar to the one in those pictures. The pictures of her love.

The doctor started to talk to herself. *Can I hug him? Can I touch him? Can I stand close to him? Is he wearing the same perfume?* The doctor went in a silent moment. The doctor went into a calming mood while she looks at those pictures.

Still, the doctor felt hopeless. She felt reluctant. She felt speechless. Moments were passing. She was still looking at those pictures. She was moving the pictures and turning them. Because the pictures were too many, they accidentally fell from her hands.

The doctor's hands started to tremble. The patient noticed that there was something on the floor. He quickly stood up. The patient got close to the doctor. He bent to the floor. He held one picture from the floor. He looked deeply in this picture. He smiled. He raised and tilted his head toward the doctor. He looked at her in her eyes.

The doctor saw the bright smile of this patient. Then the patient decided to be quick and looked back to the floor. He started to collect the remaining pictures from the floor. The patient said, "What a wonderful silent moment. What a wonderful day. What a great chance for both of us."

The patient finished collecting the remaining pictures. He stood and handed the pictures to the doctor. The doctor did not take the pictures. She was in deep silence. She took a deep breath. She tried to talk but she could not. She was looking at his eyes. She was looking at the pictures. The patient realized that the doctor was not feeling all right. He said, "Let me help you. I will put those pictures on the shelf. Do not worry, Doctor. Just go and have a seat."

Chapter Six

Doctor Mond decided to leave the clinic leaving the patient behind. She asked the nursing station to transfer this patient to another clinic. She said she felt dizzy and fatigue that she needed to go home to take a rest.

The doctor was trying to put excuses because she had some assumptions in her brain. Those assumptions were:

The patient in the clinic was similar to the love of her life.

The patient in the clinic was similar to the one in the pictures that she kept in her clinic. The patient in the clinic could be the love of her life.

Doctor Mond felt intense feelings. The doctor felt sick and weak. The doctor started to get confused. The doctor started to ask herself if he was the love of her life or if he was someone else. She started to ask herself if the love of her life is still alive or he is the one who passed away.

The doctor started to recall the meeting between her and the manager of the hospital. She said to herself, *What if the patient in the clinic was the love of my life. What if the patient who passed away was not the love of my life and the love of my life is still alive?* Tears were falling from the doctor's eyes. The doctor checked out for the day. The doctor left the hospital.

While the doctor was approaching the elevator heading to the parking lot, she started to ask herself, *What did I do? I should not leave the patient alone in the clinic. What did I do? I should not ask the nursing station to transfer the patient to another clinic. What did I do? I should have stayed in the clinic. The love of my life has passed away. I was the cause for the love of my life to pass away.*

I am guilty.

God, I ask for your forgiveness.

God, I ask for your forgiveness.

God, I ask for your forgiveness.

Doctor Mond seemed to be broken into pieces. The doctor wished to have answers for all her thoughts. The doctor said to herself, *Why I am still struggling from past events.* the doctor said to herself, *Why I am still harming myself by allowing myself to remember a pang of guilt that I did not commit.*

The doctor said to herself, *I really need support. I do not know what to do. I do not know what to do.*

Chapter Seven

The doctor went to the parking lot. She had so many thoughts. Those thoughts were rounding, rounding, and rounding in her brain. In the present time, in the past time remembering the love of her life. The doctor started the car's engine. The doctor pressed the gas pedal at an accelerating speed. The car was flying at a high speed. She was crying loudly.

She was hit the steering wheel hardly with her right hand.

The doctor seems to be not aware of the street and other cars. She feels detached from the entire world.

The doctor pressed the brake pedal hardly. Suddenly, Doctor Mond found herself that she stopped the car at a decent speed. She started to cry deeply about her losing the love of her life. She started crying that she was the cause of his death by removing the wires and oxygen from his chest.

The doctor remembered the love of her life lying on his bed weak and in a deep coma. The doctor remembered leaving the patient's room without even plugging the wires. Because the patient was in a coma.

The doctor asked herself, *Did he die, or he was alive. The one who came to the clinic looks like him. Oh, my dear God!!!* The doctor said, "He must be him. He must be him. He must be him. I must do something about it. I must go back to the clinic. I must see him. I must not lose him anymore. I must tell him how much I love him. I must tell him that I did not cause his death. I must tell him that I have here to be with him. I must tell him that I did not kill him."

Doctor Mond started to feel calm. She started to bring up herself. She started to lift her vim. She started to be more focused.

Chapter Eight

In the middle of the road, the doctor decided to reverse the road and she decided to go back to the hospital. She said, "No, no, no. I am not going back home. I need to hold on to myself and help myself by going back to the clinic and figure out was he the love of my life the one who came to the clinic tonight or not. Why should I run away?" Doctor Mond headed to the hospital. She felt calm after the shock and the tears she had minutes before.

The doctor realized that having a shock was a normal feeling when expecting a person to be dead and a day come and brings the same person who said he was dead. It was confusing.

The doctor reached the hospital. She looked at the mirror of her car. She made sure that everything was alright in her appearance. She did not appear to be angry anymore. Finally, she got out of her car completely. She stopped the car and went out of it.

Chapter Nine

The doctor headed to the hospital. She was walking in the corridor looking in front of her. The doctor seemed to be fully focused. The doctor did not want to waste any minute to reach the clinic as soon as she can.

The doctor felt worried if she saw the patient and he was really the love of her life, what would she say to him? The doctor felt worried if she reached the clinic, the clinic would be empty, and the patient would be gone. The doctor spent some time outside the hospital, and she did not know if the nursing station managed to transfer the patient to another clinic or not. The doctor seemed fully focused.

One nurse noticed that Doctor Mond was back at the hospital. The nurse tried to call Doctor Mond to stop her. Doctor Mond did not stop. She proceeded walking and walking heading to the elevator. After the elevator opened, the doctor went inside the elevator.

The elevator closed. The elevator was moving to the third floor. There was a doctor looking at her in the elevator. The elevator was moving. Doctor Mond was just staring in front of her. Her friend said, "Hi, Doctor Mond." She did not reply to the greetings.

Her mind appeared to be too busy that she did not want to speak anything but to see that patient. Doctor Mond went outside of the elevator. She headed to her office. She put her hand on top of the office door. She wanted to open the office. Doctor Mond was standing in front of the office. She looked under the door of her office. She noticed the lights were on. She said, "Who is in the office?"

It is hard to accept the fact of losing your loved one. It is hard to accept the fact of being apart from a human you truly loved. It is hard to live with the pain of missing someone. But we all believe that God has a plan for everything in life. God always puts goodness in our way and protects us from unseen dangers. God is fair.

Accepting the fact of losing someone is the first step for a good tomorrow. Accepting the fact of losing someone can help us processed our accomplishments and successes. Accepting the fact of losing someone is a blessing we acquire as we grow up.

Please always remember to push the success wheel daily honoring your success to your loved one. Those who, if still alive, would commit their life to support your success. Those who, if still alive, would celebrate every inch of your success.

I love you. But where are you so that I can tell you how
much I love you.

Huda Al Khamis

Challenges never bring negative emotions, but it shapes our success even further.

Huda Al Khamis

Lift me up with your positive words.

Huda Al Khamis

When you passed away, it feels like someone places my head under the water surface. I cannot breathe, no more.

Huda Al Khamis

I look at your videos. I look at your pictures. I talk to you often. It brings me fresh moments. I feel calm.

Huda Al Khamis

I realized that death is a must, but I promise to honor you with my success.

Huda Al Khamis

I am all yours. I am just waiting for the call from heaven
to gather my soul with your soul.

Huda Al Khamis

Purpose of the novel: inspiration of what to do when
losing your loved one
Accept, honor that love and accomplish success;
keep it up.

Huda Al Khamis

**Season Two
Door Handle**

Introduction

Like the sound of the bird. Like a clear blue sky. Like a white cloud. Like a fuggy night. Death is real. Death is clear and it comes within an unexpected moment.

To those who have lost their loved ones. To those who cry for long nights. To those who close their eyes and try to call their loved one's spirit to come over and hug them.

We all regret the days we were away from our loved ones. We all regret the days we could not make it to reach a place where a call from heaven exists to take one precious spirit (soul). We all regret old plans that kept us busy. We all mistake ourselves. We all blame ourselves to be a part of our loved ones when they wish to see us. Death cannot wait but to quickly take their souls and leave us with ton of sorrow feelings. Death is a true call but a fact to observe.

Can you imagine be in call for an emergency where you must leave everything on hand and try to catch a moment of truth. Try to catch a way to quickly go to a hospital. Try to meet your loved ones for the last time. You sure had similar moments like that. What if you arrive to the hospital and you were few minutes behind? You see everyone are there with sad faces. You are speechless. You do not know what to do.

You follow the crowd to the patient's room. That patient is your loved one. You access the unit. You hear no beep. You hear no breathe. A moment of silent. You feel weak that you cannot complete your steps toward the patient's bed. No white light. No black light. It was a call for death.

You headed to the patient's bed. You touched his head. You touched his chest. You raised his arm. You started to cry. You bend your body toward the patient. You held the patient. You left the patient and raised him toward your chest. You kept saying, "Wake up… Wake up… I am here with you. It is me. It is me."

You kept crying. You realized that this patient has passed away. You realized this patient cannot hear you. You realized it is the last time you will see this patient. You looked around you with tears in your eyes. You see people around you are looking at you. They are all sad. They are all speechless.

You kissed the forehead of this patient. You laid him on bed to die in peace. You pray his soul to rest in heaven. You checked out from the room. You wake in the hospital's corridor. You see nothing but white gowns. You wake in the hospital's corridor. You hear nothing but screaming sounds. You feel hopeless. You feel powerless.

You try to speed up your steps, but you feel your legs are too heavy. You hear someone is calling your name, but you do not stop. You keep walking. You ask yourself, *Where should I go?* You ask yourself, *Should I meet a person to talk to and cry? Or should I go to the beach and throw my sadness to the ocean's surface?*

You get into your car. You move the steering wheel. You press the gas pedal. You feel confused. You feel worried. You feel lonely. Where to go. Where to go. You keep walking.

You keep walking. Nowhere to go. nowhere to go. you close your eyes. Then you opened your eyes. You found yourself on bed. It was just a bad dream.

A bad dream can certainly impact your soul. But what would you do if that was not a dream? What would you do if what you see was real? Like I said earlier, "Like the sound of the bird. Like a clear blue sky. Like a white cloud. Like a fuggy night. Death is real. Death is clear and it comes within an unexpected moment."

Chapter One

Doctor Mond got back to the hospital. She arrived at her clinic. She entered her clinic. In her deep mind, she was eager to meet the love of her life. She was full of love, and she had a lot to say. She accessed the clinic and was about to close the door.

The office was calm. Doctor Mond felt her breath from this silence. She looked to her right, she saw no one. She looked to her left, she saw no one. She took a deep breath, and she closed her eyes for a second. Suddenly, there was a movement inside the clinic.

Doctor Mond started to feel intense. She opened her eyes. She looked in front of her. There was no one in front of her. She turned around; she did not see anyone. She asked herself, *From where does this sound comes?*

The doctor expected the love of her life to still be inside the clinic. Her assumption was wrong. Someone in the clinic said, "Hi Doctor Mond, it is me, Doctor Zeal."

Doctor Mond replied, "Oh, hi Doctor Zeal. Sorry I thought no one is in here."

Doctor Zeal said, "I met with the patient and diagnosed him. I noticed that his face was familiar, and I asked him if we met before. He told me who he is. We ended up knowing each other. We talked for a long time about his old relationship with you, Doctor Mond. Sorry, Doctor Mond. It was him." Doctor Mond started to cry and cry. Then Doctor Zeal held her friend Doctor Mond and seated her. She gave her a warm cup of water. She wanted her to relax. But Doctor Mond wanted to learn more about this meeting. Doctor Zeal kept talking…

Doctor Zeal explained to Doctor Mond about the message from that patient. "It is him, Doctor Mond. He is the love of your life. You should feel good that he is still alive."

Chapter Two

Doctor Zeal spoke to Doctor Mond about that message. Doctor Zeal said, "I received a call from the nursing station to get to the clinic and meet with the remaining patients for diagnoses."

Doctor Zeal accessed the clinic and meet with the patient. She said, "I greet the patient. I checked his file, and I started diagnosing him. There was nothing wrong but an old accident this patient had. This patient had an accident years ago. The accident locked him up. This accident simply paralyzed this patient. This patient explained that he was in job assignment in the military. He had a gun shot in his left leg that left him not able to move. This patient explained that he was sick and not able to meet anyone. It looks like he was ashamed of his current situation. He does not want any sympathy from anyone. He stayed home for years and only kept visiting his private doctor for treatment."

Doctor Zeal said, "I can understand how this patient felt. I can put myself in his shoes. I could not help it, and I cried in front of him. I was grateful to see him back to his regular life after intensive thereby, he now recovered."

Doctor Zeal said, "During diagnoses, it was clear to me that I know this patient. Guess what, he knows and remember me, too."

Both Doctor Zeal and the patient pushed and pulled old memories between the three of them Zeal, the patient and Doctor Mond.

Doctor Zeal said, "I am glad that you both will see each other. I am glad that you now will make sure that I did nothing to harm you. He left you because he was ashamed of his injury. He left you because he was paralyzed."

Chapter Three

The conversation between me and the patient was flaming high. Some moments were full of sugar talks. Some moments were bitter and ugly. Moments appeared to be in real time not in the past.

Doctor Zeal informed the patient that Doctor Mond blamed his absence, and she struggled a lot. Doctor Zeal informed the patient that he should not feel ashamed of his injury. He should not have abandoned the love of his life. He should not cause all this pain.

Doctor Zeal described to the patient how Doctor Mond missed him. She described how this impact Doctor Mond's life.

Doctor Zeal described the reaction for the patient after knowing all those sad events. He was not prepared enough to meet the love of his life when he was on bed for years. It was not an easy event for him.

The patient explained to Doctor Zeal the reason behind his absence. And how was this absence unexpected and sudden. He explained how this absence tied him on bed. He explained how he was alone that he needed Doctor Mond to support him.

The impact of this absence on this patient's soul was huge. He was not able to speak up. Doctor Mond was not able to explain his absence. Both Doctor Mond and the patient were not feeling well.

Doctor Zeal said, "Now that you know all the truth. What would you do? Are you going to meet him? Are you going to forgive him? Are you happy that he is back?"

Doctor Zeal said, "I do not see a reason why you are silent. You should be happy that he is back. You should be happy that I did not cause you a harm because I was, and I am still your close friend."

Chapter Four

Doctor Mond was still in silence. Doctor Zeal decided to proceed talking about that patient to bring Doctor Mond to the current moment. Doctor Zeal said, "The patient explained how he spent his life between the missing feelings and the struggle for being paralyzed."

Doctor Zeal interrupted the patient and said, "There was some news about the death of you and how this news changed Doctor Mond's life forever. Was that you?"

The news for the death was shocking and its effects on Doctor Mond's future. I told him you should know that Doctor Mond was fired and accused of this particular death. She said, "Now that you are sitting in front of me alive, I do not know. I do not know what is going on. I am shocked. I am confused. I am lost as my friend Doctor Mond."

The patient was silent, too. "He was here to meet with you, Doctor Mond. But he seems does not know what happened to you during all those years. It seems he does not know that he was the reason for you losing your job in that hospital. He seems not able to catch his breath and even talk. Doctor Mond, this patient is the love of your life. He searched all the hospitals to find you. He feels grateful to see you successful. He is the same person who used to empower you years ago. Doctor Mond, he believed on you. It is enough for me to read his file. It was enough for me that he did not harm you. He was sick. He was paralyzed. Doctor Mond, talk to me. Talk to me."

Chapter Five

The patient showed how sorry he feels. The patient stood up and looked at the clinic door. Then he looked at Doctor Zeal. He took a long breath. The patient said, "Look, I am here. I did not die. I am alive."

The patient explained the relationship between him and the one was hospitalized that period. The patient said, "It was me but not me. I was there but not there. The patient who passed away that night was my brother. My twin. He had a car accident in my car. He arrived at the hospital unconscious. Because he was in coma that he was not able to speak, the medical team checked his pocket. They found my ID. Then they announced that death with my name. I did not know about that accident until later. I was in a military mission. My family did not inform me about my twin brother. I did not tell them either about my accident. I spent years away from my family. I spent years away from the love of my life, Doctor Mond. I was alone."

The patient showed how he still loves Doctor Mond and he did not die that he was still alive. "He was here today to see you, Doctor Mond. He was full of joy. He was able to speak the whole story with full confidence."

The patient thanked Doctor Zeal. He asked her to send his regards and message to Doctor Mond. He explained in his message how he missed her so much and he cannot wait for both of them to meet and sit in a calm day. He ended up his talking bending his head toward Doctor Zeal asking her to excuse him for today and that he will come to the clinic tomorrow to hopefully get to meet Doctor Mond.

Chapter Six

The moment this patient checked out from the clinic was bright and full of energy. He felt calm. He felt joy. He felt happy that he was able to meet his friend, Doctor Zeal. He could not wait for tomorrow to meet the love of his life, Doctor Mond.

The patient checked out from the clinic. He closed the clinic door. He was looking at the floor and pressing hard with his both hands. He kept saying, "I will see her. I will see her. I cannot believe it that I found her. I will see her. I will see her."

The patient stayed for a couple of minutes beside the door of the clinic flying his thinking of a bright tomorrow. He closed his eyes for a while. He smiled and moved his hair from his forehead.

The patient was happy that he could at least sent his message to Doctor Mond via Doctor Zeal.

The beautiful thing with the patient that he totally forgot about his injury. He was able to shift his long-lasting bad memories into a good once.

The patient was ready to depart the hospital. He was walking in the corridor. The corridor was empty. The patient was able to sense his feet steps. The silence has covered the entire hospital.

The patient was walking and walking and walking. It was slow steps as if the patient did not want to leave the hospital. He cannot wait for tomorrow to meet Doctor Mond.

57

Chapter Seven

Doctor Zeal finished talking to Doctor Mond about everything that happened between her and that patient. And that the patient will check in tomorrow at the same time trying to meet Doctor Mond, if possible.

Doctor Mond was happy to hear that the love of her life is still alive. She did not cause his death. She did not harm him. She could still see him.

She had many questions to ask the love of her life. She could not wait to meet him. She wished that she arrived earlier to the hospital to be able to see him.

Doctor Mond thanked Doctor Zeal for her efforts. She was about to leave the clinic. Doctor Mond placed her right hand on top of the clinic door to close it. She sensed warm hand was on top of her hand.

It was quick short seconds for Doctor Mond to brainstorm who this person is. She moved her finger slightly and asked herself, *Who*? She took a deep breath. She prepared herself to turn her back to see who is standing behind her. She pressed tight with her left hand. She started to turn around. She looked at the floor. She saw the shoes for the person who is standing behind her. She was speechless. She was powerless. Doctor Mond was fully shocked.

The person who was standing behind Doctor Mond said, "Hi. It is me, Doctor Mond. I am glad to see you. I spent days looking for you coming to the clinic after you check out. But today, I think I arrived at the right time. Doctor Mond, it is a pleasure to see you. Do you have a minute to talk? I would love to chat a little with you. There is a coffee near the hospital's cafeteria. Would you like to join the table?"

As it was a shock for Doctor Mond to sense that hand above her hand, it could be a possible fresh start for her to a new start to meet her old love. It was not a planned meeting between the two of them. It was not meant to be a silent moment. It was the destiny that we all believe in.

The destiny that cheers us sometimes. The destiny that breaks us sometimes. The destiny is a written records upon God's request. We as human beings have no power to change it.

As we grow up understanding what destiny is, we can sure appreciate this knowledge and treat it as good as we could. We can take pictures with our loved ones often. We can dance with our loved ones. We can laugh loudly. We can cry with them loudly. Because we truly love them, and we can do whatever it takes to please them.

We feel calm with our loved ones as we almost forget about the pain if, God forbidden, we lost them. We should not let the negative thoughts access our peaceful mind thinking of our losses. We should keep cheering with our loved ones. We should enjoy our moments with them bit by bit, day by day and year by year.

Destiny is quick. It moves as the clock's moves. Remember that you are not the only one have losses. We all do. You feel us. We feel you. Remember that the same moment you have lost your loved ones, it is the same moment another person has a loss too in this world.

In different places, we all cry. With different reasons, we all cry.

It is density. We cannot change it. We keep missing our loved ones often. We keep crying often. But we still believe in destiny.

Season Three
Multiple Knifes

Chapter One

Doctor Mond agreed to accept the coffee hour and went to the coffee with the host. The host was Doctor Rike who used to work with Doctor Mond in her previous job.

It is a pleasure to meet you, Doctor Mond. I thought I will not be able to catch you at this time of the day. But thanks God, here we are together. I would like to thank you for your time accepting my invitation. I would like to thank you for being successful as I used to know you in your previous job.

Doctor Rike said, "I heard about your new opportunity that you started to work in this hospital. I decided to come here and congratulate you. You were among the most valuable and hard-working employees in that hospital. I am sure this hospital will reward you for being who you are. There are no specific words I can say to you to describe how valuable you are. Thank you, Doctor Mond."

Doctor Mond said, "I accept your invitation, Doctor Rike. Because you were the owner and the general manager for the previous job. I understand your reaction and how you took action to fire me after you learned about that patient who passed away. You must know that I never hurt any patient during my life. I work as a doctor because I enjoy helping patients. I work as a doctor because I have the skills that help me to do my job as a professional. I have no reason to blame you to fire me. I have no reason to hate you. You did what you should do. No more no less."

Doctor Rike said, "That was pretty much what I am here for. Now, excuse me I must go back to the hospital. I wish you all the good luck, Doctor Mond."

Doctor Mond, "You are welcome."

Rike left the coffee shop. Doctor Mond stayed alone in the shop for a little time.

Doctor Mond said, "Oh thank God. He came to talk to me. He seems to know that I did not intend to end that patient's life. I should go back home to rest. I must be prepared to meet with the love of my life. I cannot wait for tomorrow to see him alive.'

Doctor Mond went home and fall into a deep sleep. She did not know what would happen tomorrow. She seemed to be full of energy and ready to speak her feelings. She felt that she would tell the entire world that she did not kill anyone. She would tell everyone that she was innocent.

Chapter Two

The sunshine. The bird sang. The sky was full of clouds. It was 11 a.m. Doctor Mond was preparing herself to dress up and jamb to her car. She was ready to press the gas pedal and hit the road.

Doctor Mond arrived at the hospital. She accessed the elevator, pressed the third floor, and waited.

The elevator was moving toward the third floor. It reached the third floor and opened its door. Doctor Mond left the elevator.

Doctor Mond was walking in the corridor. She looked like a fresh rose that opened its leaves every morning. Doctor Mond was full of energy. She mumbled what she would say when she saw her love. She walked as a free bird free of guilt. She was now full of confidence that she was officially not a criminal. As she walked, she repeated to herself, "I will see him, I will see him."

She repeated to herself, "He is alive. He is alive. Should I hug him? Should I kiss him? I did not kill him. He must be happy to see me too."

She kept walking in the corridor. She finally arrived at the meeting place, her clinic.

She put her bag. She untied her hair. She put on her special perfume. She was well organized to see the love of her life.

She sat down near her desk. Everything seemed very silent except the clock goes tik tik tik.

She heard something like someone is knocking on the door. She jumped to the door. She opened the door. There was no one near the door. She back to her seat. She waited and waited until the end of her duty. The patient did not show up.

Doctor Mond felt worried. *Where is he? He must be excited to see me. Oh my God. Why all these things are happening now. I cannot leave the clinic until he shows up. I will stay. I will not move anywhere.*

The time was passing. Doctor Mond was still waiting. The hospital was almost empty. Only the cleaning man was still in the area. Doctor Mond was still waiting. She felt she wanted to go to use the bathroom. She went to wash her face and went back to the clinic.

She opened the clinic's door. She saw the cleaning man wiping her desk. She entered the clinic and closed the door. She approached her desk and sensed the cleaning man stopped cleaning the desk and looked at her.

She looked at him and saw his face was familiar to her. Doctor Mond was shocked. She was speechless. She said, "Is that you Riaa..aa..ch?" Clock sound tik tik tik.

The man who was wearing 'cleaning man's cloth' looked at Doctor Mond. He looked at her. She looked at him. She felt calm and peaceful. He looked wild and fired. She was speechless. She could not say a word. He placed the cleaning towel above the table. He clipped his hands to spread the dust. He sat approached her with slow steps. Doctor Mond was silent and calm.

He said, "I know that Doctor Zeal informed you about me. I came yesterday to your clinic and spoke to Doctor Zeal. I think I succeeded to trick both of you. You have no place to run away. Today is the day that I will take revenge for what you did to my twin brother."

The man turned his back and walked to the window and kept talking. He said, "Your love Rich is dead. You killed him. I said I was the one above that bed. I said I was holding Rich's ID. But what I said was false. Rich was killed by you. I am his twin brother. I searched for you for months not to sympathize with you but to take revenge. I will never forgive the guilt you committed. You ended my twin brother's life. I cannot imagine what ugly punishment you deserve. You are a criminal. You are a wild animal. You are a coward. You deserve to die."

As the man was fully attached to his twin brother's story. He kept talking and talking. Doctor Mond quickly decided to escape from the clinic. She opened the clinic's door and run as fast as she can.

The man sensed her and wanted to catch her. As he tried to run, he fell to the ground. He injured his right foot. He could not stand up easily.

He kept screaming,

"COWARD, COWARD, DO NOT RUN
NOWHERE TO RUN
I WILL FIND YOU
I WILL END YOUR LIFE
COME BACK, COME BACK."

Doctor Mond kept running. The hospital's corridor was empty. No one seemed to be in the area.

She was running and crying. She was running without shoes on her feet. She was running until she accidentally hit her left foot with a bed in the corridor. Her foot began to bleed. She was running and looking behind her. She felt unsafe hearing that man screaming and calling her.

Finally, Doctor Mond reached the main gate of the hospital. There was no doorkeeper near that door. She held the door and shook it. She held the door and hit it with her left arm.

She started to scream,

"HELP. HELP. HELP."

No one could hear her voice except the man in that clinic. He was holding his injured foot. He was in pain. But he heard Doctor Mond's screaming. He stood up and started to follow the sound of her screaming. He was trying to find her to take revenge.

Doctor Mond felt hopeless, and she was not able to hide. The main gate was locked and there was nowhere to leave the hospital. She sat on the floor with her injured foot. She began to whisper her lover's name, "Rich, Rich, help me. I am afraid. I am alone."

Doctor Mond fell into a deep sleep because she was too exhausted.

The man 'Rich's twin brother' was walking from corridor to corridor at the hospital. He tried to find Doctor Mond. The sound of screaming stopped, and the man could not follow it anymore.

The man felt angry and wanted to find a way to find her.

Time was passing and the man was left alone in the corridor. He searched for Doctor Mond in vain. He could not find her. The man did not want anyone to see him and ask him what he was doing in the hospital. The man decided to leave the hospital. His blood was all around the corridor.

He asked a cleaner man to guide him to leave the hospital. The cleaner man walked him in a side door and allowed him to leave the hospital. He went home. He took care of his injured foot. He fell into a deep sleep because he was exhausted.

The cleaning man checked the main gate of the hospital. He sensed a breathing sound. He looked behind him. He saw Doctor Mond laid on the ground. She seemed unconscious. The cleaning man touched her forehead. He realized that Doctor Mond has a high fever. He shook her face a bit. She hardly opened her eyes and said, "Rich, Rich, help me. Your twin brother is chasing me."

She had fallen into a coma.

TO BE CONTINUED

As you live in this life, you realize that what holds you
from pursuing your goals is not your spirit but your way
of thinking. Let it go, it sets you free.

Huda Al Khamis

I seldom cry. But I am your only butterfly that can reach
your place in heaven.

Huda Al Khamis

I am nearby you. I am all around you. You took my soul
when you passed away. Let me die. Let me see you. I am
waiting to see you.

Huda Al Khamis

Likewise, I am in heaven when I am with you. But I break into ice pieces when I am without you. I melt, I drain, I die hundred times. I miss you.

Huda Al Khamis

I drain when I keep thinking that I see you everywhere.

Huda Al Khamis

I have faith in God. I have faith in destiny. But destiny upsets me often. I have cracks in my soul.

Huda Al Khamis

**Destiny locks me up. I am powerless. I am hopeless.
I feel down.**

Huda Al Khamis

Destiny shows me the fact that I lost you. I look at the sky. I see a smoke. Was that the remaining of your soul? Was that your soul?

Huda Al Khamis

Have faith in God. If you feel you need to cry, cry! If you feel you need to cry, cry!

Huda Al Khamis

**Pictures of our loved ones never tied us but pushes us
and fuels us.**

Huda Al Khamis

Live the love of your lover who passed away. Feel that love as if it is fresh. Feel that love as if it is happening now (today).

Huda Al Khamis